# The Nutcracker

Retold by Emma Helbrough

Illustrated by
Anna Luraschi

Reading Consu...
Roehampt...

# Contents

A nutcracker is a wooden or
metal tool for cracking nutshells.
When this story was written,
nuts were a special Christmas
treat. Some nutcrackers were
even shaped like dolls.

## Chapter 1

# Christmas Eve

A soft, fluffy layer of snow covered Clara's house on Christmas Eve.

Inside, a party was in full
swing, but one very special
guest hadn't arrived. Clara
watched for him at the window.

4

Suddenly, there was a
loud knock on the door.
"He's here!" she cried,
dancing over and flinging
open the door.

5

It was Clara's godfather. She gave him a big hug.

"What a warm welcome on such a chilly night!" he said, with a chuckle.

Merry Christmas!

Clara loved her godfather's visits. Something magical always happened when he was around.

"I have a very special present for you this year," he told Clara, as he placed a package under the tree.

## Chapter 2

# The mystery present

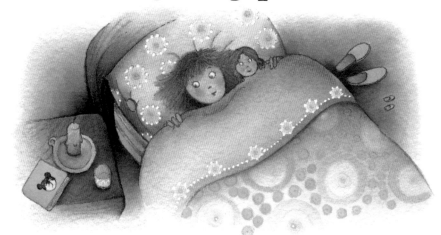

That night, Clara couldn't sleep. She lay in bed thinking about her present. "It can't hurt if I just have a little peek," she thought.

Finally, Clara tiptoed downstairs. She soon found the present, tied up with a big red bow. On the ribbon there was a tag with a message.

Merry Christmas Clara,
I hope this protects you...
With love from your
godfather x

"I wonder what Godfather means," thought Clara.

Slowly, Clara untied the bow and folded back a corner of the paper...

Inside, she found a wooden nutcracker doll, dressed like a soldier.

Just then, the clock struck midnight. Clara gave an enormous yawn. In a few minutes, she was fast asleep under the tree.

## Chapter 3

# The magic begins

Clara woke up with a start, feeling very confused. She couldn't remember where she was and her doll had vanished.

She looked around and saw she was under the Christmas tree... and it seemed to be growing.

What's happening?

But the tree wasn't growing – she was shrinking. Soon, she was as small as a mouse.

Out of the corner of her eye, Clara thought she saw something leaping around. Frightened, she darted behind a present...

...and heard the tree rustle behind her. Clara spun around.

"Don't be afraid, Clara. I won't hurt you," said a friendly voice. Clara was astonished.

But you look like...

Her doll had come to life! "I'm the Nutcracker Prince," he said, with a bow, "and I'm here to protect you. The kitchen mice are plotting to kidnap you."

The prince pulled out a
whistle and gave a shrill blow.
At once, the lid of the toy box
flew open and a long
line of toy soldiers
marched out.

Standing in rows, they saluted the prince. "Attention!" he cried. "Clara needs our help. Prepare yourselves for battle, men."

Wheel out the cannons!

Mice began to appear in the shadows. Slowly, they crept closer. Clara hid behind the prince.

"Steady, men... steady," he shouted. "Wait for the signal – and FIRE!"

Huge lumps of cheese flew
from the cannons and struck
down several mice. Some
lumps landed in the corners
and the other mice scampered
after them.

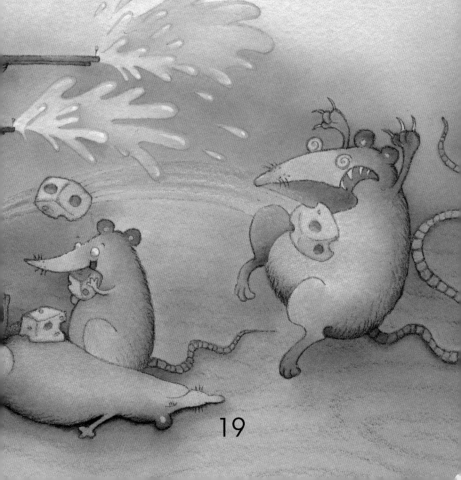

"Excellent work, men!" roared the prince, as the last mouse vanished. But the fight wasn't over yet. "Bravo," said an evil voice from the shadows.

A mouse wearing a crown and an eye patch appeared.

20

"That's the Mouse King," the prince whispered to Clara.

"Is cheese the best you can do?" jeered the king. "It'll take more than that to beat me! Now hand over the girl."

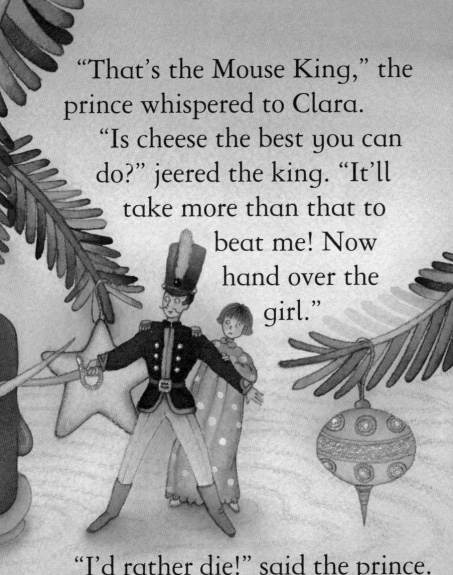

"I'd rather die!" said the prince.

"That can be arranged," the Mouse King sneered.

Soon, the prince and the
Mouse King were locked in
battle. Their swords clanged
as they danced around
the room.

Then disaster struck. The prince tripped on a lump of cheese and sprawled on the floor. Seizing his chance, the Mouse King put his sword to the prince's neck.

Well, well, well...

"I'm going to enjoy this," he said, laughing.

As the Mouse King pulled back his sword, Clara whipped off her shoe and threw it as hard as she could at his head. He fell in a heap on the floor – knocked out cold.

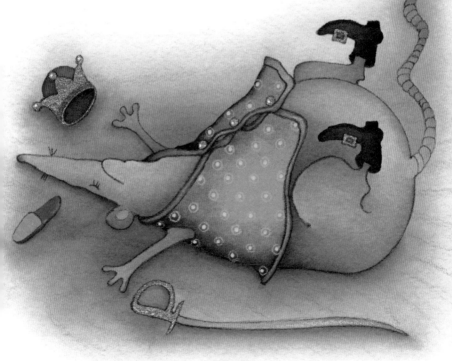

## Chapter 4

# Sleigh bells ringing

Clara rushed over to the prince. "Are you alright?" she cried.

"Yes – thanks to you," he said. "We must celebrate," he added as Clara helped him up. "I know just the place."

The prince led Clara to a golden sleigh behind the Christmas tree and helped her aboard.

"Off we go, boys!" the prince called to his four reindeer.

As they gathered speed, the sleigh started to rise up into the air. They rode out through an open window and into the night.

After some time, they came to a forest covered with crisp white snow.

"We're nearly at our first stop," the prince announced. "Hold on, we're going down!"

The snow crunched under the reindeers' feet as they landed.

Just then, a beautiful lady
dressed in sparkling white
appeared among the trees.

"Clara, I'd like you to meet
my good friend, the Ice Queen,"
said the prince.

What a lovely
surprise!

The queen led them to her icy palace, which glistened in the moonlight.

Inside, icicle chandeliers hung from every ceiling.

"You've arrived in time for the dances!" said the queen, as they walked into a grand ballroom.

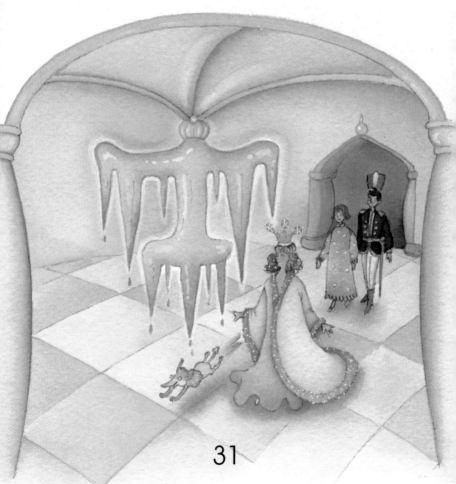

A piano began to play
and eight ballerinas dressed
in silver and white twirled
into the middle of the room.

They twinkled like snowflakes
as they spun around.

"I'll always remember this," whispered Clara to the prince, as the music came to an end.

After a game of catch with the palace poodle, it was time to leave.

"Do we really have to go?"
sighed Clara.

"Yes, we really do," said the
prince. "There's someone else I
want you to meet and we don't
have much time."

Goodbye!

# Chapter 5

# The Land of Sweets

Clara gasped when they reached their next stop. The trees were bursting with marshmallow blossoms, and lollipop flowers sprouted from the ground.

Then Clara saw that the
mountains were topped with
melted chocolate and milkshake
rivers flowed down them.

"Where are we?" she asked,
amazed.

"The Land of Sweets!"
the prince replied.

Before them stood a huge
marzipan castle, decorated
with all kinds of treats.

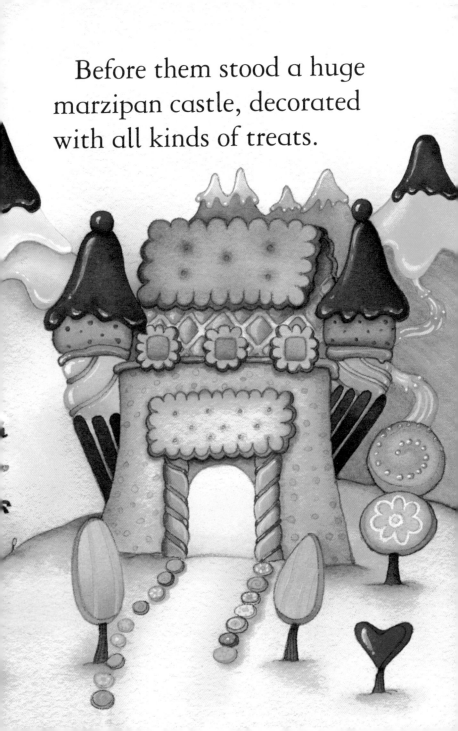

Lifting Clara from the sleigh, he set her down on the palace steps and a fanfare of trumpets rang out. At the top, the doors opened and a fairy appeared, dressed from head to toe in pink.

"Clara, this is the Sugarplum Fairy," said the prince. "She rules over the Land of Sweets."

"I hope you have a sweet tooth," said the Sugarplum Fairy, with a smile.

She led them into a grand hall, where the tables were covered with chocolate cakes, cookies and candy swirls.

"Watch the wobbly chairs," whispered the prince as Clara sat down. "They're made of raspberry mousse!"

Clara ate until she thought she'd pop.

After the feast, a band struck up and dancers from around the world performed for Clara.

First came the dance of chocolate, and a Spanish pair spun around to snapping castanets.

Next came the exotic dance of coffee. A beautiful Arabian princess danced with smooth, swirling movements in time to soft, soothing music.

The third group of dancers had come all the way from China to entertain everyone with their tea dance.

Many more dances followed, each one showing something good to eat or drink.

But the final dance was very
different. A group of ballerinas,
all dressed as flowers, performed
a slow waltz for Clara.

Their arms unfolded
gracefully like the petals of a
flower, as they weaved in and
out of each other.

"And now I'm afraid it's time for us to go home," said the prince sadly. With a sigh, Clara climbed into the sleigh and waved goodbye to the Sugarplum Fairy.

"Thank you for an amazing evening, Nutcracker Prince," said Clara, with a yawn. She was so tired that she fell asleep on his shoulder.

When Clara woke up, she was back under the Christmas tree and the prince was gone.

Only her doll lay beside her.
"Oh, it was only a dream," she cried. "But it seemed so real."

Just then, Clara spotted the tag that her godfather had attached to her present.

"I hope this protects you," it said.

"I wonder if that means he knew the Nutcracker Prince would rescue me," thought Clara. "Maybe it wasn't just a dream..."

Merry Christmas Clara, I hope this protects you... With love from your godfather x

*The Nutcracker* was written by a German writer
and composer named E.T.A. Hoffman in 1816.
Later, it was adapted by Alexander Dumas, a
French writer who also wrote *The Three Musketeers*.
In 1892, a Russian composer named Tchaikovsky
turned the version by Dumas into a ballet, which
is now performed all over the world.

Series editor: Lesley Sims
Designed by Russell Punter and
Natacha Goransky

First published in 2004 by Usborne Publishing Ltd., Usborne House,
83-85 Saffron Hill, London EC1N 8RT, England. www.usborne.com
Copyright © 2004 Usborne Publishing Ltd.